GENEVIEVE MOORE lives in Victoria, Australia.
She is an improvisational performer, voice-over artist and
has been a radio announcer and human resources consultant.
This is her first children's book.

KARIN LITTLEWOOD studied Graphic Design at the
University of Northumbria and has an MA in illustration from
Manchester Metropolitan University. She has illustrated many
successful picture books and her work has been nominated
for the Kate Greenaway Medal three times.

Foreword

This is a story about a very special girl, Catherine –
and it's a very special book too. It's warm and sensitive
about a child with disabilities, but gently subversive too.
It's a delightful positive happy story, beautifully produced and illustrated.
It belongs on every nursery and infant school bookshelf.

Jacqueline Wilson

For Catherine, her dad and her grandmother – G. M.

With thanks to Jack Taylor School for all their help,

especially Theo – K. L.

Catherine's Story copyright © Frances Lincoln Limited 2010
Text copyright © Genevieve Moore 2010
Illustrations copyright © Karin Littlewood 2010
The right of Genevieve Moore and Karin Littlewood to be identified as the author
and illustrator respectively of this work has been asserted by them in accordance
with the Copyright, Designs and Patents Act, 1988 (United Kingdom).

First published in Great Britain and in the USA in 2010 by
Frances Lincoln Children's Books, 4 Torriano Mews,
Torriano Avenue, London NW5 2RZ
www.franceslincoln.com

First paperback published in Great Britain in 2012

A catalogue record for this book is available from the British Library.

ISBN 978-1-84780-402-0

Illustrated with watercolour

Set in Berling

Printed in Shenzhen, Guangdong, China by C&C Offset Printing in June 2012

1 3 5 7 9 8 6 4 2

Catherine's Story

Genevieve Moore

Illustrated by Karin Littlewood

F

FRANCES LINCOLN
CHILDREN'S BOOKS

Catherine is a special girl
and she can do special things.

Catherine has a special walk too.

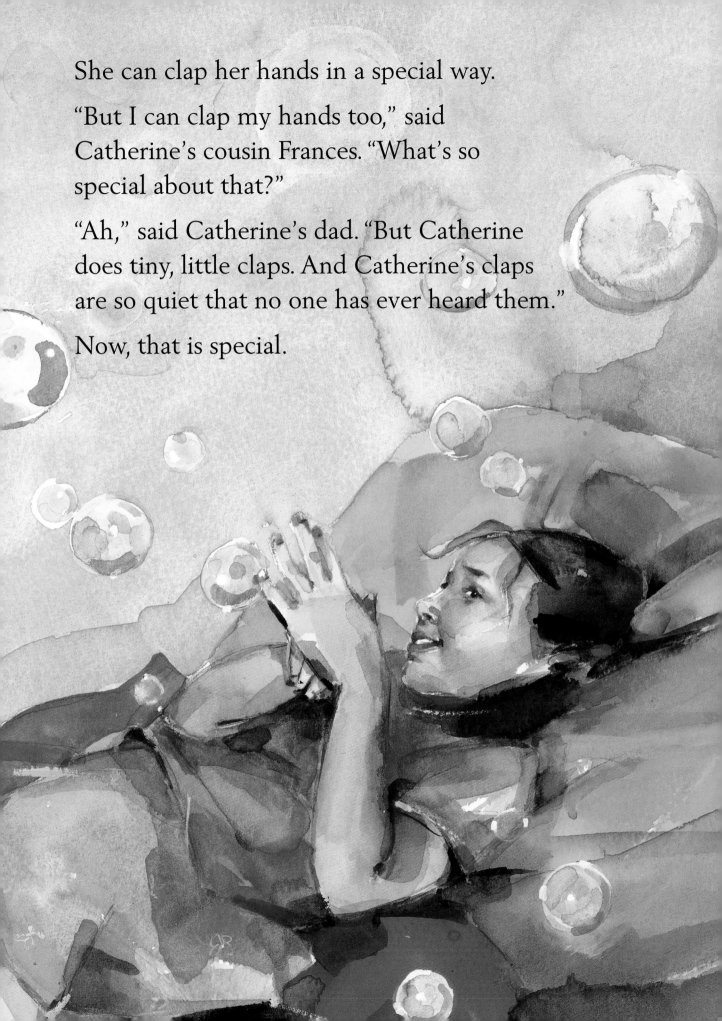

She can clap her hands in a special way.

"But I can clap my hands too," said Catherine's cousin Frances. "What's so special about that?"

"Ah," said Catherine's dad. "But Catherine does tiny, little claps. And Catherine's claps are so quiet that no one has ever heard them."

Now, that is special.

One day Frances watched Catherine walking and said, "I can walk like Catherine."

So Catherine's dad helped Frances put on a pair of Catherine's special walking boots.

Then Frances tried to walk.
She said, "See, anyone
can walk like this."

Then Frances started to wobble.
And then she began to topple,
and then . . .
she just fell over.

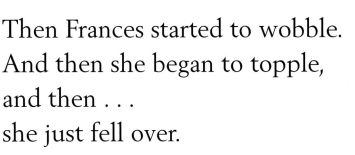

"You see," said Catherine's dad.
"Hardly anyone can walk like Catherine."

Then he helped Catherine stand up and she started to walk. Slowly and smoothly Catherine walked around in her special boots.

"But Catherine can't talk," Frances said.

"Well," said Catherine's dad. "Lots and lots of people talk. And lots and lots of people talk too much."

"Huh?" said Frances.

"Catherine listens – really, really hard," said Catherine's dad. "And that's special because hardly anyone does that."

And Catherine listens especially hard
when her grandmother is reading
stories to her.

When Catherine's dad was putting her to bed he said, "Catherine, you really are a special girl."

"You can clap so quietly
no one can hear you.

"And you can walk in special boots
that other kids can't walk in.

"And you listen really, really hard – unlike most people."

Then he smiled and said, "And it makes me feel special knowing that you are my little girl."

Then Catherine's dad kissed
Catherine on her left cheek
and then he kissed her on
her right cheek.

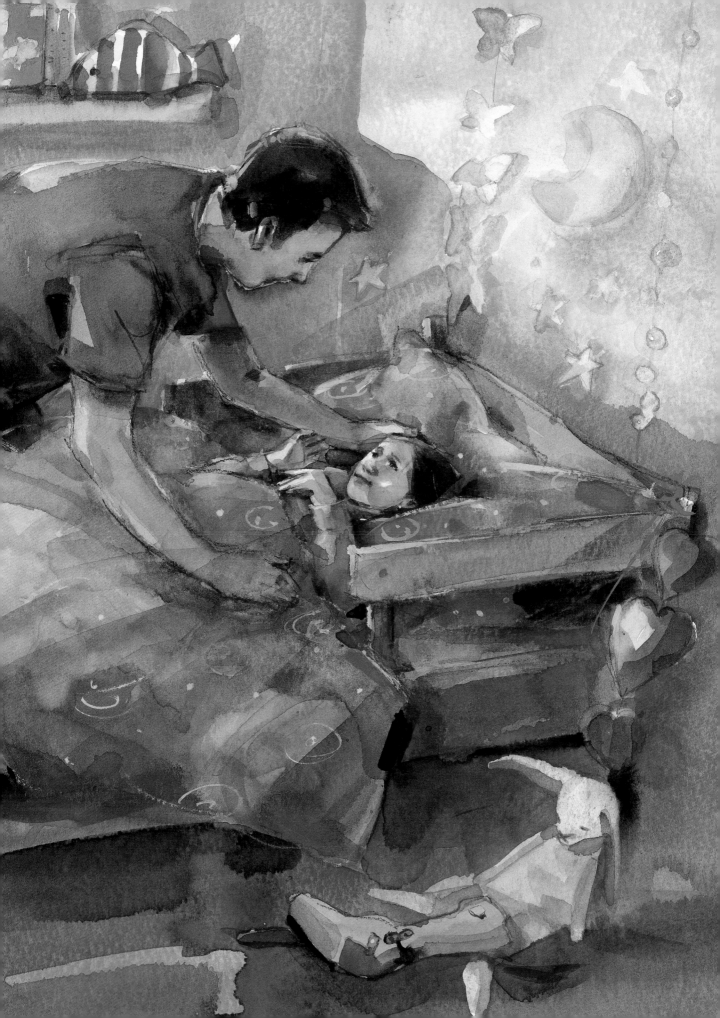

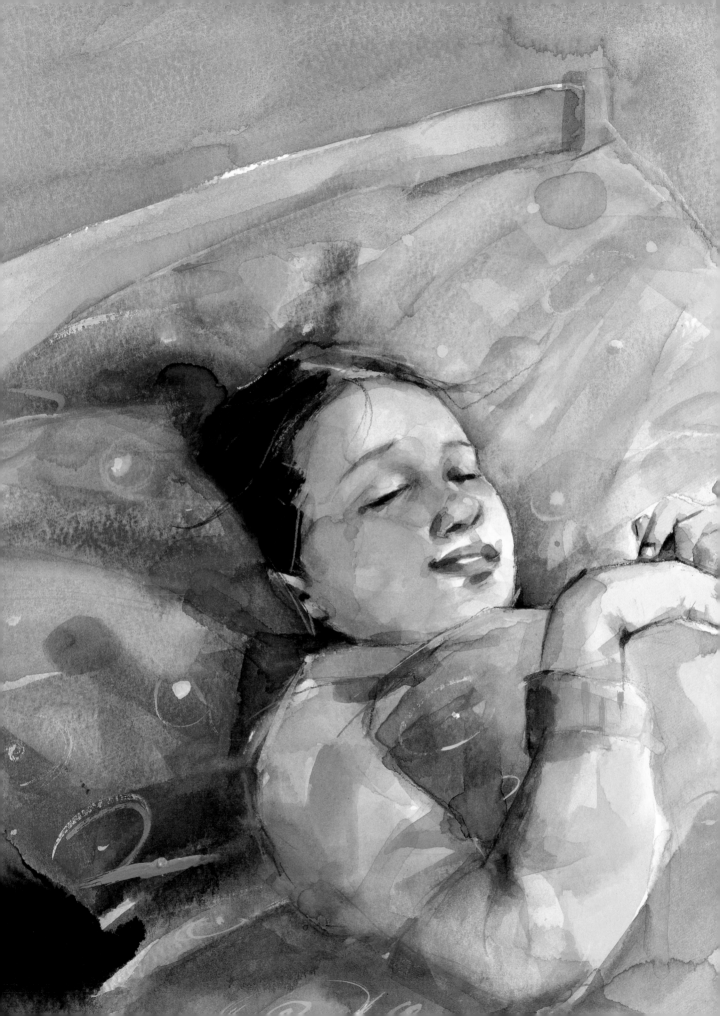

And just before he turned off her bedroom light, Catherine's dad turned around and saw that Catherine was smiling and clapping her hands very, very quietly.

Note

As an infant, the child upon whom Catherine is based suffered from a kind of epilepsy known as infantile spasms or West Syndrome. This left her profoundly and multiply learning disabled. She cannot understand a lot of what is said to her, is unable to speak, is unable to walk without the support of an adult, and is unable to perform any of the activities of daily living such as feeding herself or dressing herself.

MORE TITLES FROM FRANCES LINCOLN CHILDREN'S BOOKS

Looking After Louis
Lesley Ely
Illustrated by Polly Dunbar
"There's a new boy at school called Louis. He's not quite like the rest of us. He often just sits there and stares at the wall. If I ask him what he's looking at he just says, 'Looking at' and carries on looking."
This introduction to the issue of autism shows how Louis' classmates find a way to join him in his world. Then they can include Louis in theirs.

Hudson Hates School
Ella Hudson
"Hudson loved making things. He liked painting pictures and building models and baking cakes. He liked sewing too! But there was one thing that Hudson really hated. . . and that was school."
After another horrible day Hudson declares he will never go back to school. But one final very different test helps Hudson understand why he is special. . . and how he can learn to learn!

Hamzat's Journey
Anthony Robinson
Illustrated by June Allan
Hamzat grew up in Chechnya at a time of war. One day, on his way to school, Hamzat's life changed forever. He stepped on a landmine and lost his right leg below the knee. With the help of his family and others, Hamzat eventually reached England, to get a new leg and start a new life.
Anthony Robinson relates this true story through Hamzat's own words. It is a testament to all those who endure enormous hardship in the struggle to be safe and free.

Frances Lincoln titles are available from all good bookshops.
You can also buy books and find out more about your favourite titles, authors and illustrators on our website: www.franceslincoln.com